MR. SMALL

a big day out

Original concept by Roger Hargreaves
Illustrated and written by Adam Hargreaves

MR. MEN   LITTLE MISS

MR. MEN™ LITTLE MISS™ © THOIP (a Sanrio company)

Mr Small a big day out © 1998 THOIP (a Sanrio company)
Printed and published under licence from Price Stern Sloan, Inc., Los Angeles.
This edition published in 2015 by Dean, an imprint of Egmont UK Limited,
The Yellow Building, 1 Nicholas Road, London W11 4AN

ISBN 978 0 6035 6888 6
55642/2
Printed in Great Britain

Mr Small was out for a walk.

He was feeling more than a little sorry for himself.

It wasn't much fun being as small as he was.

He sat down under a tree and closed his eyes.

"I do so wish I was bigger," he sighed.

"Much, much bigger," he added.

Now, Mr Small did not know that there was a wizard lying down on the other side of the tree.

He had stopped for a snooze and, just as he had been dozing off, the wizard had overheard Mr Small's wish.

The wizard smiled to himself.

Without even opening his eyes, he muttered some magic words under his breath and then went back to sleep.

As Mr Small lay there, something really quite remarkable happened.

Something really quite remarkably magic.

Mr Small began to grow.

And grow.

And grow.

Until he bumped his head on a branch!

When he crawled out from underneath the tree and stood up he was taller than the tree.

Much taller.

"Gosh," said Mr Small.

He could not believe his eyes.

He could not believe his size!

He went for a walk to try out his new size.

It was wonderful.

He could see over the top of everything.

He leap-frogged over trees and jumped over rivers.

He gave Mr Uppity the shock of his life.

He was stronger than Mr Strong.

Noisier than Mr Noisy.

And taller than Mr Tall!

He could even make his fingers meet when he put his arms around Mr Greedy's tummy!

Mr Small had a marvellous day, and as the sun set he lay down in a field and went to sleep.

As Mr Small slept he shrank back to his normal size.

For you see, the wizard had cast a spell that would only last one day.

When Mr Small woke up it was dark.

"What a wonderful dream," he said to himself, and got up to walk home.

But he found he couldn't. He was surrounded by a wall!

However, when he felt along the bottom, he discovered that he could lift up the wall.

It was light outside, and when he crawled out Mr Small could not believe his eyes.

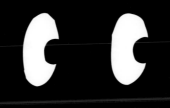

He had been trapped underneath a hat!

A hat that looked just like his own, but it was much, much bigger.

"Well, I never," said Mr Small, "Maybe it wasn't a dream after all."

That sleepy old wizard had forgotten to finish off his spell properly.

He had forgotten to make sure Mr Small's hat would shrink back to the right size.

Mr Small now had a ten-gallon hat.

A ten-gallon hat for a pint-sized person!